Humbug
Twisted Tales of Familiar Faces
Andre Gonzalez

M4L Publishing

For Elizabeth Azuero, who loved both Christmas and horror.

“Bah,” said Scrooge. “Humbug.”

— A Christmas Carol, by Charles Dickens

Presents

When the first snowflake floated down from the gloomy skies, Ebenezer Scrooge remembered the night his mother was murdered on Christmas Eve.

Scrooge stared out the window from his office on the forty-eighth floor of a skyscraper overlooking Central Park in New York City. He worked as a hedge fund manager for the highly successful firm, Cratchit and Dickens. Down below, some eight million people swarmed the streets of New York City, running around like chickens with their heads cut off to complete their last-minute Christmas shopping. If only they *were* chickens with their heads cut off. The thought brought a rare smile to the grouchy old man's lips. Vehicles sat in a jam, moving every few seconds, appearing like crawling ants from the bird's-eye view.

Scrooge enjoyed his office view, which closely resembled the same view as his apartment a few blocks away. He considered it a live look at the economy in action. All those cars and people going about their lives. Earning money. Spending money. Driving up the stock prices of various companies, where he could then capitalize and make himself even wealthier.

This time of year was best, too. Gift shopping. Christmas, Hanukkah, Kwanza, and whatever other holidays he couldn't think of. All that shit equaled a ton of dollars spent. The retailers benefitted the most, but everyone else did, too. Out shopping? Why not stop for lunch? Passing by Broadway? Why not grab a couple of tickets to a show to treat yourself after the long stressful day of shopping?

For Scrooge, gifts were a waste of money. He'd never given a gift in his life, nor had he received a meaningful one since he last celebrated Christmas over sixty years ago. Christmas itself was a sham. A dick-measuring contest where everyone tried to one-up each other with the most ridiculous presents. He'd received an annual gift from the firm for the past decade. Silly things like company branded robes, mugs, and tote bags. Things he didn't need. Not in this life. Not in any life.

Scrooge dreaded the entire month of December. The interns always decorated the office with tinsel and Christmas trees, and the whole damned place reeked of peppermint. And don't get him started on the Christmas music playing in the lobby. That was the stuff of nightmares. Just hearing Mariah Carey made Scrooge want to jump from his office window. But the fuckers didn't open, so he had to pop Tylenol in the mornings just to prepare his brain for the mess of noise that awaited.

Worst of all, so many people took time off work. Traveling. Relaxing. Eating all the cookies and eggnog like they were jolly Saint Nick himself. The fuckers. Time off meant missed opportunities to make money. And who didn't want to make money every single day? It drove Scrooge mad every Friday afternoon, knowing the stock markets closed for the weekend. Absolute bullshit.

He grew up poor and without his father, who left before baby Scrooge had even drawn his first breath out of the womb. It was just him and his mother, living in South Bronx, where she worked as a concession stand operator at the local bowling alley to get them by. The paychecks were measly, and his mother often came home in tears, carrying a bowl of nachos from the alley that she put on the table for their shared dinner. She only ever took a couple of bites, letting Scrooge eat the rest.

Young Ebenezer never pieced together his mother's misery when he was younger. But he reflected back and understood just how poor they were. The thought made him shudder. With how often crime caused local businesses to shut down in South Bronx, it was a miracle the bowling alley stayed open throughout his childhood. If it had ever closed, they would have surely ended up on the streets.

He was never allowed outside past dark, where crackheads and gun fights sang the chorus of the night. And so he stayed inside, making fake money with green markers and a pair of rusty scissors to contribute to the family income. He'd make a stack of ten one-hundred-dollar bills and hand them to his mother.

She always grabbed them with a wide smile and said, "Thank you, Ebby. This will help us eat and keep the lights on."

And while he didn't know his fake money was useless, the lights always stayed on, and he never missed a meal, no matter how light it may have been on certain evenings.

It was at this young age that Scrooge grew an appreciation for the value of a dollar. "Work hard and the money will come," his mother always said. And he now realized she was actually talking to herself. Giving herself that tiny shred of hope to push through the next day.

And so they lived like that for the first nine years of Scrooge's life. Until that fateful Christmas Eve.

The Office

"ANY PLANS FOR CHRISTMAS, Mr. Scrooge?" a voice asked, startling Scrooge out of his daydream.

He spun around and saw their newest intern, Tim. Scrooge hated all the interns this company hired, and Tim was no different. The baby-faced kid fresh out of college offered a polite smile. He was short, barely five feet tall. Scrooge had overheard some of his colleagues call the young man Tiny Tim. An insult, sure, but the boy didn't seem too bothered. Tiny Tim walked with a slight limp, but Scrooge didn't care enough to ask why.

"Christmas?" Scrooge replied. "Bah! The best part of Christmas is when it's over."

Tim's smile faded, and Scrooge noticed a file clutched in his grip. He had missed it at first, too distracted by the gaudy attire Tim considered a suit. Too much color and shimmer. The kid looked like a walking Christmas tree. Scrooge thought of hanging an ornament from Tim's earlobes for an added effect. He chuckled in his thoughts.

"What do you have?" Scrooge asked, turning his back to the falling snow outside.

"Those numbers you asked for, sir," Tim said, handing over the file with a shaky hand.

These dipshits are always afraid to come into my office, Scrooge thought.

Scrooge grabbed it and flipped it open. "Humbug Enterprises. Silly name, but lots of potential, it seems."

"Yes, sir," Tim replied. "They've increased profits the last three years by ninety percent. Each year. No one's buying them yet. People think they're growing too fast and are going to implode. No faith in their CEO."

Scrooge laughed. "He's a schmuck. I'll agree there. But the business is sound. It's worth the gamble. What do you think?"

Tim paused and gulped. Scrooge loved to put some pressure on these kids. Eventually, he'd find someone who could match his intensity and passion for money. "I agree they're worth the gamble. Strictly looking at their numbers, we'd be getting in on the ground floor of a company about to boom. I'm not even sure how the CEO could mess this up. It's not like he's out blowing money on lavish things. I've been following his social media accounts. He gets a bad rap for the things he says, but he's not as wild as people make him out to be. He's tight with his money. Still lives in a studio apartment and drives a modest car. He's worth it."

"Social media," Scrooge grumbled under his breath. He had never considered using such a thing as a resource for investing, but maybe Tiny Tim was on to something. Scrooge prided himself on being closed minded, especially toward the younger generations. But he would open that same mind if an opportunity to make money presented itself. "Very good. You may leave for the day."

"Thank you, Mr. Scrooge," Tim said, his grin returning, hand still quavering. "Have a wonderful Christmas, sir."

Being wished such an atrocity made Scrooge grind his teeth until it hurt his gums. He didn't return the pleasantries and watched the intern leave his office.

Scrooge stuffed the files into his briefcase. He had a lot on his plate, and the office would soon close. And unfortunately for him, he'd have to leave early if he wanted to grab dinner on the way home. Most places closed early on Christmas Eve, and he didn't want to get stuck eating a fast food burger like the bums he walked past on his way home.

McDonald's, Burger King, Taco Bell. Trying to be healthy in America was like trying to stay dry at a summer pool party.

But that wasn't Scrooge's concern. He picked up fresh gourmet meals from an upscale food service on his way home. A luxury of his affluence, he never knew such a service even existed until he first became a millionaire. Calling it takeout was an insult. They often provided filet mignon, fresh salmon, caviar, and pretty much anything he could order from one of the city's top five-star restaurants. After a childhood of eating bowling alley scraps, Scrooge made sure to eat like a king from the throne of his skyrise apartment.

He snapped his briefcase shut and exited his office, sure to lock the door behind him. This was always the most stressful part of his day, the walk from his office to the elevator. Especially at this time of year, when everyone was so perky and chatty. Probably because of all the time they were about to take off.

Sure, there were fewer people in the office because of the holiday, but it was still a minefield across the fifty feet between his office door and the elevators at the end of the hallway.

Susie Nash sat at her desk in the bullpen. She was the secretary, office manager, or whatever the fuck they called that position these days to make it sound less sexist. She handled all the random shit no one else ever wanted to do, and that apparently made her think she had the right to put her pointy little nose in everyone's business.

Scrooge could have taken the extra long way to exit his floor, but that would mean some stairs and an extra two hundred feet of walking that he really didn't have the time for.

So he drew in a deep breath-damn near choking on the peppermint—and took the softest steps he could manage down the hallway. Others in the bullpen looked up at him and returned their stares to their computer screens. Like normal people.

"God dammit," Scrooge muttered the moment Susie saw him and stood up from her seat. Her desk faced the hallway, so she had a clear view of every single person passing through the office. If it was up to Scrooge, he'd put her desk in the basement where she belonged.

"Ebenezer," she called out, holding up a tin container with an image of Santa Claus on the lid, laughing and holding his ridiculous gut. "I have a gift for you, from the firm. All employees get to take one home."

"Bah!" Scrooge cried out as he kept walking past her desk, not even slowing down. Another damned gift he'd throw out as soon as he stepped outside. Why couldn't the firm just save the money on such useless things and reinvest those funds into the market? And if they were so insistent on spending that money, why not just give everyone a twenty-dollar bonus? At least they could do what they pleased with the money and not have an impractical coffee mug sitting in the cabinet at home.

From the corner of his eye, he watched Susie hurry around her desk and burst through the bullpen with the container gripped tightly by her chunky fingers.

She had too much energy. Every day of the week. Susie was short and plump, her perfume always sprayed on too thickly. Her scent made Scrooge nauseous, and everyone could always tell when Susie had ridden in the elevator because the stench lingered for a good thirty minutes after.

"No time, Susie," Scrooge said, continuing down the hall at a pace too rapid for a man of his age. He raised his hand and realized he needed to slip his gloves on. "Have places to be."

"It's no worry, Ebenezer," she replied, panting for breath as she jogged to keep up beside him. "If I have any extra containers, they'll just throw them out. I don't care what you do with it, but just take it."

Scrooge reached the elevator lobby and pressed the call button, dreading that it could sometimes take two minutes for the car to arrive. But it was his lucky day, and the chime rang out only fifteen seconds later.

Susie forced the container into Scrooge's hands, leaving him no choice but to take it into the elevator. What a bitch!

"Have a merry Christmas, Mr. Scrooge!" Susie called out as the elevator doors closed and cut off her friendly waving. And that fucking smile.

"Merry Christmas," Scrooge mocked in return once he was alone with his thoughts. His curiosity never left, so he fumbled with the container to take the lid off, immediately snapping it back shut when he saw two dozen cookies waiting inside.

"Bah!"

When the elevator reached the bottom, after stopping four times during the descent to crowd the elevator, Scrooge tossed the container in the first trash can he saw, glad to rid himself of such filth. Not even the bums outside were worth giving free cookies to.

He strolled across the marble floor of the building's lobby, briefcase in hand, eager to have dinner so he could get back to work upon his return home. Scrooge lived only two blocks from the office, in a different skyscraper with a similar view to his office. He enjoyed the view of Central Park, but rarely found himself there. Too many people. And nature. Lots of Christmas trees and lights around this time of year, too.

Scrooge approached the first intersection outside the office building and crossed the street with the cluster of business people in fine suits. Nothing like the cheap and flashy crap Tim wore every day. When he reached the other side, a homeless man sat against the wall of a café, holding out a paper cup and shaking it at everyone passing by, humming some incoherent tune under his breath.

Seeing this made Scrooge's blood instantly boil.

"Can you spare a buck?" the man asked Scrooge. "In the name of Christmas."

Normally, Scrooge raced by these people and paid them no attention. But considering the time of year, and the bum bringing it up, Scrooge couldn't just keep on walking.

He stopped and crouched over, catching a whiff of the man's repugnant body odor.

"Why don't you get off your ass and get a job like every other functioning member of society?" Scrooge said, gritting his teeth. "What makes you think you can sit here and ask for free handouts?"

The homeless man only stared at Scrooge, his brown eyes bloodshot and glossy. The paper cup wavered in his hand, just like the papers Tim had passed over.

"I was on the brink of homelessness once," Scrooge said in a lower tone. "And you know what I did?"

The man shook his head, fear creeping into his bulging eyes.

"I worked my ass off," Scrooge said, teeth gritted. Spit flew as he spoke, but he didn't care. Maybe the bum would enjoy the shower. "And now I'm one of the richest people in this city. Grew up with no parents. No support. Just me and my own determination. People like you are offensive to the very fabric of our society. Anything is possible, and you choose to sit here like an idiot all day!"

Scrooge looked into the paper cup, saw a dollar bill and a handful of coins. He spat into the cup and stormed down the sidewalk, rejoining the crowds without another word.

There was a time shortly after his mother's death when the sight of a homeless person brought terror to young Scrooge. But throughout his adolescence, Scrooge had channeled that fear into hatred. It was impossible to go through life without seeing a homeless person, especially in New York City. He knew if he ever wanted to become something, he'd have to kick his greatest fear aside.

So he did. And he never looked back.

He continued the rest of his walk home, fists clenched tight enough to turn his knuckles white. His thoughts spiraled. *I should have taken the bum's cup. Or at least smacked it out of his hand.*

Scrooge hated wasting an opportunity to prove a point. He was so consumed with his thoughts, he walked right past the food service he had intended to stop in. His appetite had vanished. The encounter made him want to go to the office in his apartment and find ways to make more money when the markets opened again in two days.

He *had* made himself from nothing, and any reminder only further fueled his motivation. There was no such concept as "enough" for Ebenezer Scrooge. He wanted more. Always.

When he reached the sidewalk outside his apartment building, Scrooge looked up at the tower he called home. Eighty levels high, he felt like a God living up near the clouds. He cracked a rare smile as he admired the building he and his mother had only seen from a distance all those years ago.

The grin disappeared as quickly as it had come, and Scrooge started toward the entrance, a glass rotating door. But he froze as he approached, disturbed by what he thought was his mind playing tricks.

Standing in front of the entrance, dressed in a silk suit no different from the one Scrooge currently wore, was Jacob Marley, Scrooge's longtime business partner. The last person he had ever considered a friend.

It was him alright. Youthful appearance despite his age. And handsome. That determination swimming behind his intense facade. The same determination that told Scrooge they were cut from the same cloth.

But there was only one problem with what his eyes were seeing.

Jacob Marley was dead.

It Can't Be

"Marley?" Scrooge said, looking around. No one was paying them any attention. "How...why...what is this?"

Marley smiled. He looked the same as when Scrooge had last seen him. Pristine teeth. Full head of thick gray hair. Handsome. Marley always got approached by the ladies when they went out for drinks. That was a lifetime ago. Back when life had joy in it.

Perhaps Marley had gotten off easy with his early demise. For Scrooge had faced the cruelty of aging into his golden years. He was never as appealing as Marley, but lately Scrooge refused to look at the shriveled-up monster who now appeared in the mirror. His face seemed stuck in a perpetual snarl, hair turning whiter with each passing week.

"Scrooge, my dear friend," Marley said, throwing out his arms and pulling Scrooge in for a tight hug. He smelled of the same cologne he used to wear. Jovan Musk for Men. Marley always kept two full bottles of the stuff. "You didn't think I'd actually stay gone forever, did you?"

Scrooge felt his throat dry up. Part of him wanted to laugh and jump for joy. Another part wanted to cry and run to the nearest mental institution.

"Marley," Scrooge said, tightening his grip on the briefcase. "You're dead."

Marley laughed. "Ahh yes. Such is life. Death isn't the end, Ebby, but only a new beginning. We used to tease all those others who believed such an absurd idea. But it turns out *we* were the ones who had it wrong."

Only two people had ever called him Ebby. And both were dead. Yet, one stood in front of him and used the nickname that sent chills down his back.

"So you're a ghost?" Scrooge asked, eyes watching Marley for any sign he was part of his imagination. "Or some illusion my mind has made up. But how? I haven't thought about you in years."

"Now, that's not very nice, Ebby," Marley scoffed. "I think about you every day. But I suppose that's because I have little else to do. Can you believe there is no stock market in the afterlife? What these people do for fun is beyond me. Gets quite boring, actually. But I found my way out, and you were the first person I wanted to come visit."

Got out? Visit? Marley made it sound like he had just escaped from prison.

"You're not real," Scrooge repeated, rubbing his forehead like it would make this dream go away. But it wasn't a dream. He had felt Marley's hug. Breathed in the cologne. Heard the chatter of all the New Yorkers parading around the city. Even smelled the damn peppermint scent oozing from inside the building lobby—why was that smell *everywhere*?! Dreams didn't have that many details.

"I'm plenty real," Marley said, his grin unwavering. "But you're right. I am a ghost. My body is still dead as a doornail, but they couldn't keep my spirit away. Can we talk in your apartment? No one else can see me, so it might look odd if we keep this up right here."

Several people had walked by Scrooge, who appeared to converse with himself, on their way into the building. Realizing this, he nodded silently and entered. He paid no attention to the giant Christmas tree in the lobby. Didn't hear the holiday music blasting through the speakers as he hurried to the elevator. Mariah Carey herself could have been singing into a microphone and Scrooge wouldn't have noticed. His mind raced with confusion and panic.

None of those things mattered right now.

Scrooge broke into a complete jog during the last stretch to the elevator and pressed the button a dozen times in rapid succession. Marley strolled along at a calm pace and joined Scrooge's side just as the doors parted.

A group of people filed out before Scrooge and Marley stepped in. They were the only two during the ride up to the sixty-seventh floor.

"Why are you here?" Scrooge asked, keeping his gaze forward, not wanting to look at his dead friend. Surely he would disappear eventually. Vanish back to where the hell he had come from. "None of this makes sense."

The elevator hummed as it began its ascent. If it made no stops, the ride took exactly ninety-four seconds. Scrooge knew this because time was money. He had made forty-nine dollars per minute according to his tax returns last year, and he always thought about the roughly seventy-five dollars that were missed out during each elevator ride.

But today, he was getting his money's worth.

"I'm here because I'm your friend, Ebby," Marley said, examining his ghostly fingernails. "You've been too focused on work. You need to have some fun. And what better time of year than Christmas?"

Scrooge grunted.

"I know, I know," Marley said, raising his hands. "You hate this holiday, and I don't blame you one bit. But what if you could do something fun on Christmas? Something not even related to the holiday. You're going to have the day off each year. Imagine if you actually had something to look forward to when it comes around."

"What the hell are you talking about, Marley?" Scrooge asked. "The entire world shuts down for Christmas. It's quite the selfish holiday. It assumes everyone wants to celebrate."

"I'm not here to discuss the intricacies of the holiday. Only to provide you with some food for thought. Are you still in good shape these days? You look rather thin, but I suppose that's easier to fix than if you were five hundred pounds."

"I'm fine," Scrooge grumbled. The elevator stopped, doors parting to reveal a long hallway. Scrooge's floor only had two doors. One which belonged to his apartment, the other to a neighbor he had never actually seen.

Scrooge hurried down the hall and unlocked the door on the left. Part of him wanted to slam the door on Marley and head straight for bed. Surely he needed to sleep off whatever the hell was happening. He'd heard of people having mental breakdowns from too much stress. While he'd never openly admit to feeling stressed, the current events were causing Scrooge to second guess everything he believed about himself. Perhaps the hunger for more had finally caught up to him.

He didn't slam the door, instead holding it open just long enough for Marley to shuffle in.

Marley's eyes widened as he looked around. "This is quite the place you have, Ebby. Your apartment before was incredible, but this one's on a different planet."

Marley left the foyer and passed through the kitchen on the right, stopping in front of the refrigerator. "I've heard about these," he said, lowering his face to the smart panel. "A fridge that talks back to you, right?"

Scrooge nodded, eyeing the knife rack on the countertop. He didn't know exactly how much to trust this ghostly version of his old friend.

He watched as Marley paraded around the apartment, admiring the millions of dollars worth of art hanging on the walls. An original van Gogh, Picasso, and O'Keeffe. He had won each through auction houses.

Marley ran his fingers over Scrooge's piano, tapping a couple of keys to let the tune ring out across the silent apartment.

"You don't play the piano, Ebby," Marley said.

"It's for decoration," Scrooge replied.

"Such a classy man! And sophisticated. Who else would have a piano like this? Is it even real?"

"It better be," Scrooge said, crossing his arms. "I paid a million dollars for it."

"A *million*?" Marley asked, raising an eyebrow. He stood up straight and planted his hands on his hips. "You know, Ebby, this apartment looks like it was set up for hosting events. All the open space. The famous art. A kitchen that would make a world-class chef drool. But the Scrooge I know would never host an event. Can you imagine two hundred people in here having the time of their lives?"

Scrooge shook his head. "I suppose there was a time where I imagined hosting glamorous events here. I've made so many people rich that I assumed they'd want to spend time with me. But I just don't know how to connect with people outside of business. Sure, I don't necessarily *want* to, but I figured I'd have a few friends by now."

Marley grinned and shuffled over to Scrooge. "Oh, Ebby. I'm probably the one person who knows you best. You are far from friend material. I'm not talking about your relationship with me, but with the world. You're hard. Never let anyone close. You assign a dollar value to every person who comes into your life. That's just not how normal people operate. Not sure how I slipped through the cracks."

"You never feared me," Scrooge said. "Everyone else drops silent the moment I enter a room. They avoid eye contact."

Marley shrugged. "You're intimidating. And that's why I liked you. Never took bullshit from anyone. Always knew exactly what you wanted in life and went for it. There's not enough of that in this world."

"Then why don't you stop bullshitting me and tell me what you're doing here," Scrooge said.

Marley nodded. "There he is. Okay then. I'm only here to warn you, as my dear friend. Others are coming for you, Ebby. Tonight. When the clock strikes nine, you'll be visited by another ghost. Then two more will follow. They're going to take you places and give you opportunities never imagined."

"Ha!" Scrooge cried, throwing his head back. "Three other ghosts? I must be dreaming. Or dead. That's it. I'm dead and this is all a sick prank you're playing on me in the afterlife."

"Tell yourself what you must," Marley replied calmly. "But you're not dead. And you're completely awake. Now tell me you'll be ready to have an open mind when these ghosts arrive."

Scrooge let out a nervous laugh. "Are they going to ring my doorbell and ask to come in? This is preposterous."

Marley sighed. "I know you're a man of reason, Ebby. But you must open your mind. If you don't, you'll get nothing out of these visitors tonight. And you'll wake up tomorrow full of regret. Christmas is already a rough day for you. Don't make it worse than it needs to be, okay?"

Scrooge rubbed his temples. With each passing second, it was growing apparent that he wasn't going to wake up from this nightmare.

"Okay," he said. "I'll talk to your ghost friends."

Marley pointed at Scrooge. "Not my friends. They're completely different from me. Less chatty. Taller. Uglier. But they will help you. I can promise you that. You'll want to resist them at first—that's normal. But they only want to make your life better. Remember that."

Marley wandered back toward the door.

"And when will I see you again?" Scrooge asked.

Marley reached the door and stopped, his back to Scrooge. He spun around to face his friend. "I'm afraid this is it, Ebby. I must be getting back. Was quite risky coming all this way, but I had to warn you. For your own sake. You're still my favorite friend, Ebby. I wouldn't have risked myself if you weren't. I just hope you'll think of me at least once in the next ten years."

Scrooge didn't know what to say and stood frozen as he watched Marley pull open the door and step out to the hallway. Just before the door closed, Marley called out, "Follow your heart, Ebby!"

Scrooge stood alone in his silent apartment, staring at the clock hanging on the kitchen wall. It was already five o'clock.

Baked Cookies

Scrooge spent the next four hours trying to take his mind off the ghosts that supposedly would soon show up at his apartment. He poured two glasses of scotch and tried to work in his home office. The numbers on the reports may as well have been hieroglyphics. Working no longer seemed important.

At six o'clock, he considered going for a run. Maybe tonight would be better spent in Central Park. Anywhere besides his apartment. But Scrooge didn't know all the details. Were the ghosts coming to his apartment, or to *him*? If he had to encounter ghosts, it may as well be within the familiarity of home. He imagined running through Central Park, chased by ghosts that no one else could see. Someone just might call the police on him for unusual behavior.

At seven o'clock, Scrooge paced circles around his dwelling. Seeing Marley's excitement for all his possessions reminded him he actually had incredible artifacts on display. Three paintings worth almost half a billion dollars, and he had never really stopped to admire and appreciate them.

Vincent van Gogh was a master of his craft, and it always blew Scrooge's mind when he remembered van Gogh had only sold one painting during his lifetime. How could a man with so much talent go through life without making a living from said talent? Dedicating an entire life to a hobby seemed impractical. But he did it, and he never got to see the recognition he received after his death.

At eight-thirty, Scrooge went into the bathroom and splashed water on his face. He hadn't looked at himself in the mirror in several months. Not truly. And he now saw the haggard lines of age webbed around his face. Crow's feet. White hairs curling out of his nose and ears. He looked like a tired old man, but felt far from it.

"Maybe I'm dying," he whispered to himself. "That must be it. Not dead, but *dying*. This is some sequence of hallucinations that happens before you pass. I've heard of this."

The thought made Scrooge's gut sink. He couldn't die tonight. He still had so much work to do. Money to make. *The money isn't going to make itself.* He had said that in a meeting once, and his colleagues had a custom metal poster made with the saying on it, gifting it to him for Christmas four years ago. That was the closest thing he'd received to a decent gift.

He'd shown no appreciation and tossed the poster aside. That's when the silence and awkward stares at work really elevated to another level. Scrooge had done this to himself. Made his life this way.

Why couldn't he have just said thank you like a normal person? After Marley had passed away, Scrooge had to grow comfortable knowing he was likely going to die alone. He had no connections beyond that friendship. And he hadn't thought of Marley in the past decade because the memories only made him feel like shit, reminding him of the inevitable conclusion that awaited his own life.

If he had just been more open to those trying to be kind to him, maybe he would have a party happening right now, instead of another cold, silent night alone.

But it was too late for reconciliation. Not if Scrooge was to die tonight. All he could do was fight whatever ghost came through his door. Or wall. Or whatever the fuck was going to happen.

The clock was approaching nine, but Scrooge had avoided looking at it. It could be any minute now, and part of him still wanted to bolt out the door and run down every flight of stairs until he reached freedom.

He was in decent shape, but not enough for all that.

When Scrooge finally left the bathroom, he returned to the kitchen and reluctantly checked the clock.

It read 9:02.

A flutter filled his chest. The ghost of Marley had been joking with him. His night could proceed as normal.

Right when he thought of returning to his office to pour another glass of scotch, the lights in the apartment flickered three times in rapid succession.

The momentary hope vanished from Scrooge, replaced by sheer panic.

"Hello?" he called out, only getting an echo in response. "Show yourself. Face me like a man, you chickenshit."

The lights stopped flickering and grew brighter. So bright, Scrooge thought they might burst. The temperature inside elevated, like someone had set half the apartment on fire.

But there was no fire.

Just as everything seemed to reach a literal boiling point inside, the lights shut off, leaving Scrooge in complete darkness. The temperature swung the opposite direction, and suddenly Scrooge could see his own breath with each terrified exhale.

His heart hammered in his head, making it difficult to listen through the silence. *What the hell kind of game is this?*

He stepped silently toward the knife rack on the counter and grabbed a chef's knife with a shaky hand.

"You won't get away with this!" Scrooge shouted into the void. Only the ambient glow from Manhattan shined through his window, providing just enough light to see the knife glimmering in his grip. "Too many people will come looking for me. They'll find you and make you pay."

Saying this out loud only made Scrooge feel worse. He knew it was a lie. No one would look for him. If he didn't show up to work on the twenty-sixth, how long would it take for anyone to notice? Or rather, to care he was missing?

Considering the way he had treated his colleagues, he imagined some of them were eager to have Scrooge out of their lives.

"The old man not here again?" they would ask after finding his office empty for a third consecutive week.

"Maybe he fell down a manhole!" another would say. And they'd have a nice laugh about Scrooge's well deserved fate.

The temperature continued to fall, making Scrooge's teeth chatter as the rest of his body joined his already quivering hand.

Banging came from the hallway outside, like someone was running down the corridor, punching the walls with each stride. The noise shifted inside, and all the doors in the apartment started slamming shut, then opening and slamming again.

"Get the fuck out of my apartment!" Scrooge shouted, but the symphony of doors and loud bangs drowned out his voice. It sounded like several people were pounding his walls now.

This only lasted for ten seconds before the apartment returned to deafening silence. Once it did, Scrooge squeezed the knife and stepped out from the kitchen, looking down the dark hallway toward his office and bedroom.

A shadowy figure appeared at the end of the hallway, consumed by the surrounding darkness. It swayed like a tree in a gentle breeze.

Scrooge narrowed his eyes to make out this creature, assuring himself it was the ghost he'd been forewarned about and not something concrete.

It grew larger, taking up more of the hallway. But Scrooge realized it wasn't growing; it was approaching him. *Gliding* toward him. The creature's head nearly scraped the hallway's ceiling, which was ten feet tall.

It entered the living room, dressed in all-black robes, hovering six inches above the floor. Scrooge looked up at the towering figure, which he assumed was looking back.

It had no face, only a pit of darkness where its face should have been. It raised a lengthy crooked arm, and from beneath the black robes extended a long, skeletal finger. Pointed right at Scrooge.

"No!" he shouted., taking a step back, squeezing his fingers around the knife's handle.

The creature moved toward him with no urgency, drifting above the floor. Scrooge had backed up to the door when the creature was within six inches. He swung the knife, jabbing and slashing with all his might. But the blade only sliced *through* the creature and didn't seem to bother it in the slightest.

The ghost glided backwards a few feet, hovering in front of Scrooge. And still pointing.

"What do you want?" he cried out, tossing the knife aside. "If you're the reaper, just take me already. Don't torture me!"

The ghost made a motion that looked like a head shake. It approached Scrooge, even slower this time, as if it wanted him to trust it. The finger lowered.

Scrooge panted for breath. Sweat streaked down his face and back. Somewhere in his mind, he envisioned his grave stone. Standing tall and immaculate in a cemetery where not a single soul would ever visit.

Here lies Ebenezer Scrooge. A man of great wealth.

That's all he was. He had no other purpose in this world.

The ghost extended both arms like it wanted to hug Scrooge. His legs locked from the terror coursing through his veins.

Two bony hands reached out from the robes and fell gently on each of Scrooge's shoulders. The instant they made contact, the temperature dropped even more. Scrooge felt like he was lying naked in the Arctic Circle. But the sensation only lasted a few seconds. The room grew darker until it became pitch black.

In the darkness, he felt like he was spinning. Tumbling up and down as if on a roller coaster.

When his feet hit solid ground a moment later, something thumped Scrooge hard in the back and everything returned to normal.

Well, somewhat normal.

The temperature and lighting were natural. Only Scrooge was no longer standing in his apartment building. He wasn't even in Manhattan.

Scrooge studied the building in front of him and recognized it at once. He looked down to see the cracked sidewalk beneath his boots. To the left stretched a long street block full of criminals lingering in the night.

The ghost reappeared next to Scrooge and only hovered, looking straight ahead.

Snow was falling, and the faintest scent of baked cookies oozed from the building in front of them.

"Why am I here?" he asked, eyes bulging at the sight of his childhood apartment. The brick facade. Shattered windows with bars over them. A puzzle of lights turned on up and down the building's six floors. Gun shots and sirens wailed in the distance. How many nights had he fallen asleep to those exact sounds?

Then he realized it was that night.

The night.

Inside that apartment, his Mom prepared a feast of roast chicken, canned green beans, and mashed potatoes. Cookies baked in the oven while they ate their luxurious feast that only happened twice a year. Christmas Eve and Scrooge's birthday.

His mother played their raggedy radio on the kitchen counter, Christmas music all day and night. Burl Ives sang "A Holly Jolly Christmas" while they both hummed along between bites of dinner.

"I was able to get you two presents this year instead of one," his mother said with a satisfied grin, sucking a clump of potatoes off her finger. "Plus Santa will be bring you one. I'm sure of it. You've been such a good boy this year, Ebby. I'm proud of you. Straight A's. And your teachers all say you're a math wizard."

"Three presents this year?!" young Scrooge cried, turning around in his chair to look at the three-foot-tall Christmas tree standing in the corner of the living room. Sure enough, there were two presents under the tree, wrapped to perfection in a shiny paper that looked completely out of place in an otherwise dreary apartment with brown walls, floors, and furniture. "You're the best mom in the whole world!"

His mother had giggled at the statement, tears welling in her eyes. It was the last time he heard his mother laugh, a sound that echoed throughout his memories all these years later. Thinking of these moments before his world flipped upside down was the closest Scrooge felt to warmth in his typically icy heart.

When they finished dinner, Scrooge passed the dishes to the sink while his mother opened the oven and pulled out a sheet of cookies shaped like reindeer, Santa, and candy canes. Tubes of frosting were piled on the countertop for their fun night of cookie decorating that awaited.

The scent of those cookies filled Scrooge's nose and nearly lifted him off his feet. He drooled at the thought of eating one. Forget the frosting. He just wanted to eat the whole sheet of cookies.

That's when a soft knock came from the door.

His mother frowned as she looked at the clock on the stove. "That's weird. We're not expecting any guests. Who would be out in this weather?"

She placed the tray of cookies on top of the stove and clapped her hands together. "Probably someone at the wrong apartment. Happens a lot this time of year. People from out of town come to visit."

Scrooge watched as his mother shuffled out of the kitchen and turned the corner, out of sight. It was just him and an unattended tray of freshly baked heaven.

There were so many cookies, he couldn't count them fast enough. At least twenty. Probably thirty. His mom wouldn't notice if he ate just one. Right? Being young, his ambition made him believe he could actually get away with eating the whole sheet before she came back into the kitchen. Blame it on a squirrel. Or a rat.

Scrooge licked his lips and tiptoed toward the stove, happy to be in his slippers that were silent when he stepped carefully enough. The cookies watched him approach, tempting his senses. He had to act quickly, not wanting to leave any trace of evidence of his pending crime.

So he snatched the first cookie he could reach, a Santa one. And just as he stuffed it into his mouth, his mother let out a horrific shriek from the other room.

Scrooge's blood froze. Nearly choking on the cookie, he spit it out onto the floor. He knew she wasn't screaming at him. She wouldn't have gotten *that* mad about a cookie. His mother was in trouble. He dashed into the next room and saw a man standing in their open doorway, a black gun pointed at his mother's face.

The man looked over at Scrooge and smiled. Scars and scabs covered the man's oily face. He wore three layers of jackets, each tattered with holes and stains spread about. He had scraggly facial hair and cracked, pale lips containing traces of dried blood. And his teeth, or what remained, were black and yellow, and rotting. Stringy gray hair matted flat against his scalp, chunky flakes clinging to the ends as if they were afraid to fall off. He reeked of piss and cigarettes.

"Ebby," his mother said in a whisper, eyes dancing back and forth between her son and the man. "Go to the other room and don't come out until I say."

But Scrooge never moved. He heard the panic in his mother's voice and refused to leave her side.

"Go on, boy," the gunman grumbled, waving the gun in his mother's face. Just seeing that made Scrooge want to jump up and choke the man. But he was grossly outsized and had no chance.

Scrooge still didn't move. He wasn't sure he *could* if he wanted to. His legs were locked, throat swollen shut. He couldn't speak.

The gunman looked back at Scrooge's mother and shrugged. "Forget the kid. Just give me everything you have."

"Please," his mother cried, her arms fluttering out of control. "It's Christmas Eve. I'm just trying to have a nice holiday with my boy."

"I don't give a shit what you're trying to do, lady," the man said, sounding almost bored. "We all got mouths to feed."

"Please," his mother repeated. "Come back next week when I get paid, and I'll give you money. You have my word. Just please leave us alone tonight. I promise I'm good for it."

The man cracked a manic grin. "I don't need no money next week, lady. I need it right now. *Tonight*. What are you not understanding?"

He whipped her across the face with the gun, drawing blood and a whimper.

"Mom!" Scrooge shouted, taking two steps toward her and stopping as soon as the gunman turned his weapon on him.

"Stop right there, boy," the man snarled.

"Leave my mom alone!" young Scrooge yelled, surprising himself with his lack of fear despite having a gun pointed at him. He didn't even look at the gun. Just imagined being the hero. He could slide and try to kick the man's knees. But the man wouldn't even feel the kick from his size six tennis shoes.

"Cute kid, lady," the man said, holding his crazed grin steady as he swung the gun back to his mother.

Scrooge looked at his mother and saw fresh tears gliding down her cheeks. Her lips shook. He'd never seen fear on his mother's face before this night, and it would be an image burned into his memories for many years to come.

"I don't have anything of value," his mother said, drawing in deep, calculated breaths. "I promise. Come back next week and I can help."

The man drew in a sharp inhale. "Smells like you're eating good in here. Stop bullshitting me. Give me the presents under the tree."

His mother took a step back, shielding the tree with her body as she spread her arms out wide.

"I'll be damned if you take these presents," she said through gritted teeth. Her fear gave way to an unwavering confidence upon hearing this request. "I've been saving all year to get my boy these presents. If you think you can just come in here and take them, you're out of your mind!"

The man looked at Scrooge, gun still pointed at his mother. For a split second, Scrooge thought the man was overtaken with compassion and was going to leave. Instead, he pulled the trigger.

With catlike reflexes, the man lunged to the tree and snatched one present—a large box—before Scrooge's mother had even collapsed to the floor. He bolted out of the apartment, leaving Scrooge alone with his dead mother.

She hit the floor knees first and landed on her back, lifeless eyes staring at the ceiling. A round hole appeared dead center on her forehead, blood pooling from the back of her skull. Scrooge wept as he buried his face into his mother's chest, praying to whoever would listen to bring her back.

But it was done. Scrooge lost his mother, half of his presents, and innocence in a matter of seconds.

All while the smell of cookies filled his nose. And Burl Ives continued to wish him a holly, jolly Christmas.

The Silver Revolver

"Why did you bring me here?" Scrooge asked the ghost, his bottom lip quivering as he played the events of that night.

But the ghost only hovered and faced the old apartment building.

"On the anniversary of this night I've tried to erase from my memory!" Scrooge shouted. "And you bring me here?!"

His mind was racing to piece together how all of this could have happened. He was just standing in his apartment seconds ago. How did this ghost teleport him to a different borough?

I must have hit my head. Yes! I swung the knife and missed the ghost, hit my head on the wall, and now I'm here. My body is still in my apartment. This is all part of my imagination. Suppressed thoughts.

But the scent of the cookies was too strong. And the familiarity made Scrooge's stomach twist with angst. Just like with Marley, this wasn't some illusion or dream. This was really his childhood apartment. The cold air stinging his lungs was as real as it gets.

But his mother was dead. The scent of cookies had to be part of his imagination. A suppressed memory. Just because it smelled like his mother's cookies didn't mean it *was* his mother's cookies.

He looked down the street again and noted the cars parked along the curbs. They were all from the 1950s. No sports cars. No electric vehicles that had become the buzz of his modern time.

"This is impossible," Scrooge said to the ghost.

The ghost made that shaking motion with its head again.

"Are you going to speak?" Scrooge asked, receiving the same response and growing rather irritated.

His fear of the ghost had completely worn off. If it had wanted to kill him, that would have happened by now. And it certainly wouldn't have gone through all this trouble of bringing him here.

"Are we in the 1950s?" Scrooge asked, looking around to make sure no one was passing them by. He had seen plenty of people talk to themselves while living in this neighborhood, but he was not one of them. Especially after all these years.

The ghost nodded slowly and confidently.

Its face remained cloaked in darkness, and Scrooge could only feel coldness each time the creature breathed down upon him.

"Is this..." Scrooge began, but had to regain some composure. "Is this the night it happened?"

The ghost raised its hand and pointed at the first window on the right of the apartment building's front entrance. On the other side of that window was the old apartment he lived in with his mother. Where she was murdered.

Scrooge never thought he'd return to this place. Yet, here he was, against his will.

He drew in a deep breath, the cold air biting his lungs. He intended to stroll up to the window and take a peek inside. But the thought of seeing himself, and his mother, on the night that changed everything was too much.

The ghost held its finger pointed at the window, unbothered by Scrooge's dilemma.

After a minute, Scrooge mustered the courage to take a step toward the apartment building. He already knew what was on the other side of the window, so why the need to look at it? Why did people insist on slowing down to gawk at an accident on the side of the road?

Curiosity was perhaps the most irresistible desire in the world. Even a man as cold as Scrooge couldn't resist the urge.

He grumbled and took five more steps toward the apartment building, and moments before he reached the window, a gunshot rang out from inside, the sound piercing Scrooge's heart through the layers of memories he had stuffed over this event.

It all came rushing back. The music playing in the background. The cookie he had shoved into his mouth. His mother lying dead on their living room floor with a bullet hole in her head. And that son of a bitch bum taking his present from under the tree and running out of the building.

Yes! Scrooge thought, instantly spinning to his left.

Sure enough, the bum burst out of the building with the present clutched under his arm.

Adrenaline pumped into Scrooge's veins.

The bum clearly wasn't too worried about being followed, as he slowed down upon reaching the sidewalk. Because of Scrooge's proximity to the window, the homeless man never noticed him as he exited the building and turned in the opposite direction.

Scrooge looked at the ghost, which remained in the same spot. Instead of pointing at the window, it now pointed at the man trailing down the sidewalk.

"Is this real?" Scrooge asked. "Am I supposed to go after him?"

The ghost said nothing. Nor did it move.

When Scrooge woke up this morning, he certainly hadn't thought he'd have the chance to chase down his mother's killer. The man responsible for the pain and anguish Scrooge had carried throughout his entire life.

But just as he never shied away from taking a chance on a new company making its initial public offering, Scrooge salivated at the opportunity in front of him.

He broke into a jog and followed the bum. Normally, his joints would creak and pop in protest—Scrooge had zero interest in wasting his precious money-making time on something like fitness. But being in the past, he felt invincible. Like he could run through a brick wall.

Scrooge no longer worried about the thugs loitering on the block, and they paid him no attention as he passed them by. He looked over his shoulder once to see if the ghost was following him. It was, but remained several paces behind.

Once the bum reached the end of the block, he turned right onto Jackson Avenue, a block of local businesses that included a barber shop, dry cleaners, a butcher, and a bodega. Scrooge had frequented this area as a child. Picking up laundry, grabbing ingredients for dinner, and, in the incredibly rare instance, getting a haircut.

He didn't have time for nostalgia, too consumed following the man with his present. A gift he had never known, but now he suddenly *needed* to know what was inside.

The man turned down an alley, and Scrooge's heart thumped harder. The alley stretched back fifty feet, lined with dumpsters on either side. But the most important thing Scrooge noticed: the bum was alone.

A sense of destiny swooned over Scrooge. Just him and his mother's murderer. This man had a gun, but Scrooge didn't care. The bum hadn't even seen him.

He still had his back to Scrooge.

This is your chance, idiot! Go!

Scrooge wasn't entirely sure what he would do once he came face to face with this despicable human, but his legs started anyway. He walked at first, then jogged, and finally was sprinting as he approached the bum.

The hobo must have heard the pounding footsteps because he stopped and looked over his shoulder. But he was too late.

Scrooge jumped toward the man, arms sprawled out, and brought him crashing to the ground. The box flew out of the man's embrace as he hit the pavement with a hoarse grunt.

"You piece of shit!" Scrooge shouted, swinging wild fists. "Rot in hell!"

He'd always suspected a lot of his built-up aggression stemmed back to this night, and living through it a second time proved that true. The bum whimpered and raised his arm over his face to block the blows from Scrooge.

"Where's your gun?" Scrooge screamed in the man's face.

He stood up, pulling the bum up by his three jackets, and slamming him against a nearby dumpster.

The gun clattered to the ground, and Scrooge caught enough of a glimpse to see it land between the man's feet. Scrooge dove for the gun before the man realized what had happened, too dazed from his head crashing into the dumpster wall.

As Scrooge scrabbled for the gun, the bum fell onto him, his weight pressing into Scrooge's back and pinning him to the ground. But Scrooge already had a grip on the gun, a silver revolver.

He only had to fight to turn his body halfway around and that gave him the window to whip the gun across the bum's face.

Blood instantly shot out of the man's nose as he wailed, both hands clapped over his face. He rolled off Scrooge, who stood up and pointed the revolver at him.

"Get up, asshole!" he shouted. "Get up right fucking now!"

The man parted his hands to reveal blood smeared all over his face. His eyes narrowed on the gun, fear swimming beneath the surface.

"Get against the wall," Scrooge demanded, and the man backed against the brick facade of the building behind him. "Do you know who I am?"

The man raised his trembling hands, eyes wide with fear.

Scrooge stepped forward and pressed the barrel of the revolver into the man's forehead. "I'm that little boy whose mother you just killed."

He spat on the bum's face, not moving the gun. The man said nothing.

Rage had completely filled Scrooge, every fiber of his being on fire. How badly he wanted to keep pressing this gun into the man's head. Keep pressing until it punctured his skull and touched the wall on the other side.

"Why did you kill her?" Scrooge shouted, pressing harder. "What was the point? Why couldn't you just have taken the present and run? I still needed my mom."

Tears streaked down the bum's face.

"Oh, now you want to cry?!" Scrooge cackled. "I don't fucking think so."

He pulled back the gun and smacked the bum across the forehead with it. The man's head jerked to the side, and a fresh stream of blood oozed from the wound.

"I'm sorry, mister," the man cried. "It wasn't supposed to happen this way. I got scared and pulled the trigger."

Scrooge laughed as he brought the gun back up and aimed it at the man's face. "Scared? You break into my family's house to rob us, and *you* got scared? No one was threatening you. This is South Bronx. It's not like the police would have even showed up if my mom called them. You had no reason to pull that trigger."

"I know," the man cried, still holding his hands up. "I made a mistake."

"Well then," Scrooge said, cocking the revolver. "I guess I'm going to make one, too."

He pulled the trigger and watched as the man's brains splattered across the brick wall. They say revenge is never the best option, but seeing this sack of shit slide down the wall, lifeless, brought a level of closure Scrooge never thought possible.

"I got him, Mom," he whispered to himself. The urge to laugh grew too strong and Scrooge couldn't contain it. He stared at the dead man on the ground and felt a profound sense of accomplishment. Like it was something that had been on his to-do list for the last five decades and he *finally* got to cross it off.

Blood had splattered across Scrooge's face after firing the gun, and he licked it off his lips. To say he enjoyed the taste would be unseemly, but he didn't give a shit. He *loved* the taste.

"I just made the world a better place," Scrooge said to the dead body now lying in a lump on the ground. "Because you're no longer in it."

He kicked the dead body in the chest. Then the head three times, laughing throughout the process like a child running through the sprinklers.

Scrooge looked to his left and saw the present lying unattended, its shiny wrap glimmering in the dark.

"After all these years," Scrooge said as he shuffled toward the present and picked it up with both hands. It was rather light despite its bulkier shape. "I finally get to see what you got me, Mom."

Scrooge looked around the alley. The ghost hovered at the end, like it was standing guard to give Scrooge his privacy for this intimate moment. Had it been there the whole time?

He didn't care right now, and ripped open the present.

Beneath the wrapping paper was a cardboard box, shaped like a perfect cube. Scrooge pulled at the flaps until the tape tore apart. He looked inside and gasped.

"Oh, my God," he whispered, pulling out a black top hat. "I always wanted you."

Eavesdropping

Scrooge returned to the ghost waiting at the end of the alley, his new top hat worn proudly.

He was maybe six years old when he had first seen the Disney version of *Alice in Wonderland,* and instantly grew fond of the mad hatter and his signature headwear. All Scrooge had wanted as a child was a hat just like it. And now it fit him perfectly as an adult.

His mother had always bought his clothes several sizes too large, so he'd have time to grow into them. They didn't have the budget to get new clothes every year, so she used this approach and sent Scrooge to school in baggy clothing for a couple of years at a time. She apparently did the same when buying the top hat. It would have drooped over his entire face had he worn it as a child.

Still, he was grateful for the gift all these years later, and wearing it woke a distant part of his inner child. Scrooge was on the verge of laughing as he marched down the alley. Life was actually pretty good. He had his new top hat. His mother's killer was dead.

"That went splendidly," he said to the ghost.

The ghost only gave its slow nod before reaching its bony arms out and placing its hands on Scrooge's shoulders, just as it had done to bring them into the past.

"Not again!" Scrooge cried. "I'm just getting started!"

But the ghost, as it had proven, answered to no one.

So they went on their somersault through the darkness. Scrooge held his hat as they tumbled through the void of time and space, worried it would fly off his head.

He landed back in his apartment kitchen seconds later. Alone.

Scrooge felt above his head, relieved the hat had survived.

"Ghost, are you there?" he called out. But the apartment remained silent. The ice maker in the freezer clattered to life, startling Scrooge, who spun around ready to throw more fists. He laughed at himself when he realized the source.

"Was that it, ghost?" he shouted. "Are we done for the night?"

This time, a knock on the door responded.

No one knew where Scrooge lived. Now that he thought about it, there had never been a knock on the door as long as he lived here. He always met food delivery people in the lobby. Packages were sent to his mailbox in the building's basement. His supposed neighbor would be the only other person to step foot on the same floor, but they may as well have been the ghost for all Scrooge knew.

They never greeted Scrooge. Didn't bring over a fresh pie to welcome him to the floor. A quiet neighbor who kept to themselves. Just the way Scrooge liked it.

"Who goes there?" Scrooge said to the door.

The knocking came again. An identical cadence, neither harder nor softer.

"Did you get stuck outside, ghost?" he asked, shuffling toward the door. "I thought you could just go through walls."

Scrooge's confidence was soaring. He was on top of the world and ready to welcome whoever the hell waited on the other side.

When he pulled the door open, however, he jumped back and let out a startled laugh. The creature standing in the hall looked like the ghost he had just visited the past with, only it was much different.

Gone were the black tattered robes, replaced by well-kept red robes. The last ghost was tall—Scrooge stood eye level with what would have been its stomach. But this new ghost was taller. He was eye-to-eye with the ghost's knees—assuming it had a body structure similar to humans.

From the doorway, he couldn't see its upper body.

"Stand back, ghost," Scrooge said, inching toward the door. He stepped out and looked up at the ghost's hooded head, which nearly scraped the ceiling in the hallway.

"Are you the same one that just took me into the past?" he asked.

The ghost shook his head, much harder than the previous one.

"I am the ghost of Christmas present," the creature replied, causing Scrooge to jump. It had a deep baritone, booming voice.

"Goodness!" Scrooge cried. "Wasn't expecting you to speak. You look just like the last one that was here, only bigger."

"That was the ghost of Christmas past," it replied. "That ghost was to show you where you came from."

"Sure did," Scrooge replied, grinning. "And it gave me a chance to make things right."

"If you insist," the ghost replied. "Come, we have little time."

"Where are we going?" Scrooge asked, refusing to move any closer to the ghost.

"We have to make one quick stop. You're too trusting of those in your life."

Those in my life? Scrooge thought. *There is no one in my life.*

The ghost started spinning. Much like the Tasmanian Devil in those cartoons, just not as fast. It became a red blur and widened its funnel to engulf Scrooge. He looked around, seeing only spinning red walls before the darkness swallowed him up for a second time.

This trip didn't have the tumbling sensation, but one of a free fall. His guts felt like they were going to come out of his throat. But the feeling only lasted a moment, and they landed on the ground, the red ghost back to its normal state.

They were on a sidewalk again, but not in the Bronx. Scrooge wasn't sure where exactly they were. Maybe somewhere in Queens or Brooklyn. In front of them was a concrete path leading up to a house.

"Keep in contact with me," the ghost said, reaching out its long, skeletal arm like it was waiting for its prom date to grab hold before they entered the dance, "and you'll remain unseen."

"Unseen?" Scrooge asked. "Where the hell are we?"

"You shall see," the ghost said. "Come."

Scrooge reluctantly grabbed the ghost's arm, noting how it felt like nothing more than a broomstick beneath the robes.

The ghost floated toward the house, bringing Scrooge along. They went right through the brick exterior and were standing in the corner of the dining room. A couple sat at a table, two candles lit between them as they faced each other. They each had a glass of wine and plates filled with baked chicken, diced potatoes, and asparagus. The room smelled heavenly.

Scrooge didn't recognize the woman at the table, but knew the man at once.

"Tim?" Scrooge asked. "Tiny Tim from the office. Why are we here?"

"Listen," the ghost replied. "For once in your life, silence yourself and listen."

"You didn't have to wait so late for me to eat," the woman said.

Tim smiled. "Don't most people eat dinner at ten o'clock? I kid. But I'd never leave you to eat alone. It's part of being with a nurse, and one I'm willing to accept."

The woman chuckled. "So did anything interesting happen at work today?"

Tim sighed and poked at his chicken. "Just another glamorous day working for the most miserable man in the world."

"Again, Timmy?" she said. "When are you going to tell him off?"

"Tell him off?" Tiny Tim asked. "Ebenezer Scrooge? I know you haven't met him in person, but he's as bad as I've described. Probably worse. If I told him off, I doubt he'd even notice. The old bat only hears what he wants. All he cares about is money. Quite sad, actually. I get it. We work in finance and deal with millions of dollars every day. But the guy acts like money is literally the only thing in the world."

"He must do something for fun," the woman said, taking a sip of wine. "I highly doubt he just comes to work, then goes home and sleeps until the next morning. There is always more than meets the eye."

"I'm not sure there is," Tim said. "I've tried starting conversations with him. About stuff not work related. The weather. The Yankees. Don't even get him started on Christmas. He absolutely despises the holiday. He actually gets offended when it's even mentioned."

"Does he have any pets?" the woman asked.

Tim shrugged. "Doubtful. If he did, I'm sure they'd jump out of that skyrise building he lives in just to be spared from belonging to such a sick, cruel man."

"Weren't you going to invite him over?" she asked. "Try to break the ice."

"I was going to," Tim said, "but there's no use. I went into his office just last week to ask about his Christmas plans, and he lost his shit. Threw a stapler across the room and told me to get the hell out. I'm telling you, everyone hates him. He's nothing but a black cloud in the office. Sucks the joy out of every room he steps into. The only reason he still works there is because of the insane amount of money he brings in. I'm sure the partners don't like him, either, but they've left him alone all this time. Funny enough, he treats everyone in the office like they are a walking dollar amount. Naturally, he thinks most of us are a waste of company resources. But the partners treat him exactly the same. Maybe that's just how this industry is."

"Everyone has common ground you can find," the woman replied. "Some are just harder than others."

Tim nodded before taking a drink of wine. "Well, at least I don't have to see him for two days. Hope he gets trampled by a pack of carolers while he's out spreading his misery."

The woman laughed. "Oh, Timmy, you're too funny."

The ghost pulled Scrooge back like a parent yanking its toddler out of a dangerous situation. Together, they moved through the walls and were standing back outside. The ghost let go of Scrooge and glided a couple feet backward.

"Is this how everyone really feels about me?" Scrooge asked. "They hate me?"

"It appears so," the ghost replied calmly.

"Well, I hate them, too!" Scrooge cackled. "What was the point of this, ghost? I've never given two shits what those people at the office think about me. They're all just jealous they don't have my bank account. My apartment. My life."

Now that he thought about it, it made perfect sense why Scrooge hated the people he worked with. They had no drive or ambition to reach the same level of success as he had. They were perfectly content collecting their measly paychecks, riding the subway, and returning to their little homes outside of Manhattan. Scrooge had an insatiable thirst for more, never understanding how anyone could live differently.

"So, why did you bring me here?" Scrooge asked. "You want me to ruin Tim's night?"

The ghost nodded. "Make it right, Ebenezer. People hate you because they don't understand you. If you remove people who don't understand you, that will leave more people who do. What is Tim providing for the world? Not as much as you."

Scrooge cracked an evil grin. "I understand, ghost."

Dinner with Friends

SCROOGE MARCHED UP TO Tiny Tim's front door and knocked.

The door creaked open to reveal a surprised Tim, eyebrows elevated to the top of his forehead.

"Mr. Scrooge," Tim said, looking over his shoulder inside the house. "What...why...?"

Scrooge raised a finger. "Never mind all that, boy. I've come to make amends. Want to make things right. Mind if I come in?"

Scrooge forced what he believed was a cheery voice and felt like an idiot for speaking in such a higher pitch.

Tim looked inside again, flustered. "Uh, okay. Sure. Come in."

He stepped aside and allowed Scrooge to enter the house. The red ghost waited on the sidewalk, floating around without a care in the world.

When Scrooge had first entered the home with the ghost, he hadn't felt the warmth from the heater running at full blast. But now he did, and it was plenty welcome after standing out in the cold for so long.

"Are you hungry, Mr. Scrooge?" Tim asked. "My girlfriend prepared dinner. We just sat down to eat."

"Girlfriend?" Scrooge replied, entering the dining room where the woman stood up from her seat, eyes as wide and shocked as Tim's. "A pleasure to meet you."

The girlfriend stuck out her hand, and they shook. "I'm Erica, sir. Tim's told me so much about you."

Scrooge kissed Erica's hand because it seemed like something a decent person would do. Her cheeks flushed at the unexpected contact.

"I'm sure he has," Scrooge said, letting out a chuckle. "Seems like lots of people from the office have plenty to say about me. But I suppose it's deserved."

"Let me fix you a plate, Mr. Scrooge," Erica said, spinning around and disappearing through the kitchen door behind the dining room.

Tim pulled out the open seat between him and Erica, and Scrooge sat down, shifting several times to get comfortable on what felt like a hard log beneath his ass.

"I can take your hat if you'd like, Mr. Scrooge," Tim offered.

Scrooge waved him off, but knew he needed to play polite. "No need for that...thank you."

"How did you find where I lived?" Tim asked, genuinely curious.

"Company records," Scrooge said. "Quite simple, really. I have you interns do a lot of the work on the computers, but I can still get around fine on my own."

Erica returned from the kitchen with a full plate, glass of wine, and a fork and knife wrapped in a napkin. She set up the meal for Scrooge before returning to her seat at his left.

"I see," Tim said. "Well, what brings you all the way out here on Christmas Eve?"

Scrooge cleared his throat and picked up his silverware. The fork was thick and heavy. The kind they used at expensive steakhouses. He poked around his plate, not hungry despite blowing off dinner, but eager to try what looked like a delectable dish.

"Well," Scrooge said, putting down the silverware and grabbing the glass of wine for a quick drink, "it's been brought to my attention that I come off a bit rude to everyone in the office. And I don't mean to be. My job is incredibly stressful, and I'll admit I let it get the best of me."

Tim's jaw hung open like he had just seen Santa Claus running naked down the street. Erica stuffed food into her mouth and appeared content to sit back and watch this exchange.

"That's incredibly thoughtful of you to stop by, Mr. Scrooge," Tim said. "I really appreciate it."

Scrooge waved him off. "It's nothing, really. I figured what better time of year to make things right."

"Indeed," Tim said with a wide smile. Scrooge couldn't wait to wipe that stupid look off his face.

"Say, Tim." Scrooge leaned in and lowered his voice. "Do you mind me asking why you walk with a limp?"

Tim exchanged a glance with Erica across the table. She nodded to reassure him.

"I suffer from a mild case of cerebral palsy," Tim said. "I have a good treatment plan that allows me to function regularly. So the limp is really the only negative I still have from it."

"Interesting," Scrooge said, crossing his hands. He ignored the food on his plate, his mind too consumed with the endless possibilities in front of him. "So I assume running is rather difficult for you."

"Running?" Tim repeated. "Afraid that's not an activity I'll get to do as long as I live."

Scrooge picked up his silverware, moving the knife to his left hand. "Tell me something else, Tim."

"Anything, sir," Tim replied.

"Why did you wish for a pack of carolers to trample me?"

"Excuse me?" Tim asked, his eyes fluttering as they looked back at Erica.

"Don't play dumb with me, *Timmy*. You wished a group of carolers would trample me while I spread my misery. That's a direct quote from you."

"I...didn't say that," Tim replied, worry now overtaking his face.

"Okay, I think that's enough for tonight," Erica said.

Scrooge whipped the steak knife to his left and slashed Erica across the throat in one clean motion. Both of her hands shot to her throat, blood bursting out like a fountain. It splattered across Scrooge's face and landed on his top hat.

Tim shrieked and kicked himself away from the table. Erica made gurgling sounds as she stood up, spun around twice with her eyes bulging, and collapsed to the floor in a lifeless heap.

"What the fuck?!" Tim shouted. He had fallen out of his chair and scooted away from the table on his bottom.

"Tiny Tim," Scrooge said, licking his knife clean of Erica's blood. "You said I suck the joy out of every room I walk into. Figured I may as well live up to my reputation. Would you say I'm doing a good job here tonight? AM I?!"

Tim backed into the wall and struggled to climb to his feet.

"I didn't mean any of that," Tim cried. "I was just venting. Like everyone else does after a long day at work."

Scrooge threw his head back and laughed, rising from his seat with the knife still in his grasp. "Venting? I don't think I've ever done such a thing. That's the problem with you kids. You have these beautiful jobs that pay you enough to live a comfortable life. And what do you do? Complain about it. I'm not saying every day is a walk in the park at the office, but every day at work is one that provides. You should be so lucky to have a job that allows me to maintain my lifestyle. Where is the gratitude from you little shits?"

Tim struggled to his feet, using the wall to propel himself upward. "I don't know what you're talking about!"

Scrooge reared back and threw the knife at Tim. He'd never thrown a knife in his life. Had never even played sports to gain a basic understanding of throwing. But it soared across the kitchen, spinning end over end, before landing squarely in Tim's thigh.

Tim shouted, his hands clutching for the knife and yanking it out. He threw it back toward Scrooge, but it went sailing past his head. Blood streamed from the wound and turned Tim's light blue pants dark.

"I can handle disagreements in the office," Scrooge said, taking a casual step toward Tim, who remained with his back against the wall. "That's part of business. But to wish death upon me. Well, that's just cruel. Wouldn't you agree, *Tiny* Tim?"

Tim nodded hurriedly. "Yes, sir. I apologize. I only said those things out of frustration."

Scrooge stopped and grabbed his glass of wine from the table. "Apologies won't get you out of this, Tiny. It's too late. You said what you said. And since you said it in the confidence of your home, you meant it. I'm going to gut you like a fish."

Sweat poured down Tim's face, his skin glistening beneath the dining room's bright lights.

"Mr. Scrooge, please," Tim begged, raising his hands. "I'll quit the firm. You'll never see me again. I promise."

Scrooge threw his head back and laughed. "Like I'd fall for that. And what, you're just going to help me bury your girlfriend's body and pretend I never killed her? I'm not stupid, Tiny. You're the only witness to her murder, so that leaves a natural resolution to make sure you never say a word."

Tim pressed harder into the wall behind him, as if he could break through the drywall and bricks and run—no, limp—to freedom outside.

Scrooge stepped closer to Tim and was bracing for the boy to fight. But he only quivered, like he'd already accepted his fate.

Chickenshit.

"I'll do whatever you want," Tim said, just above a whisper. "I'll help you clean up her body. Lie to the police. Tell them she left me and went to Europe. It doesn't matter. You don't need to kill me."

Scrooge took a long swig of wine, then tossed the rest over his shoulder to have an empty glass.

"You're just a coward, Timmy," Scrooge said. "I know a pig when I see one. And you'll squeal the first chance you get."

He took another step closer, now within four feet of his target.

"No, Mr. Scrooge," Tim pleaded one final time. "I'll leave the country. You have the money to make me go away. Send me to the most remote place in the world and I'll stay there 'til my last breath. I swear."

Scrooge grinned and smashed his empty wineglass on the edge of the table. He held it up, admiring what remained. Jagged, sharp edges were still attached to the stem, which he gripped tightly.

Tim's eyes grew as he, too, looked at the new weapon Scrooge had just formed.

"I don't know if they have internships in the afterlife," Scrooge said, "but I highly suggest you don't talk badly about your own boss!"

Tim screamed and threw his body toward Scrooge. The shout caught him more off guard than anything, but Tim could only move so fast. Scrooge had plenty of time to react and jammed the wineglass into Tim's gut.

Tim still had enough momentum to knock them backwards, the top hat flying off Scrooge's head as they went down. They hit the floor, Tiny Tim on top of Scrooge, blood seeping from his lips.

Scrooge still hadn't loosened his grip on the wineglass, and pressed it even deeper into Tim's abdomen.

"Shame isn't it, Tiny?" Scrooge said. "I actually liked you. Thought you had a bright future in finance. Not quite a younger version of myself, but close."

Tim's body trembled, and he gurgled on his own blood.

Scrooge pushed him up and rolled aside just before Tim vomited a shocking amount of blood. He stood up and brushed himself off, grabbing his blood-covered top hat and placing it back on his head.

Tim fell to his back and looked up at Scrooge, reaching out with a desperate hand.

Scrooge knelt down and clasped his hand like they were best friends saying hello. "Sorry, Timmy. I know you want me to put you out of your misery, but I much prefer to let you suffer a slow, painful death."

Scrooge let go and stood back up, throwing the remnants of the wineglass on top of Tim's convulsing body. He strolled to the door and opened it, pleased to find the ghost still waiting patiently outside. Before he stepped out, he looked over his shoulder and said, "A merriest of Christmas to you, good sir."

Mirror, Mirror

"Well done," the ghost said when Scrooge returned to him on the sidewalk.

Scrooge winked at him and tipped his hat. "A pleasure."

"You clean up well, sir. Are you ready to return home?"

Scrooge raised his eyebrows. "You're asking me? The last ghost gave me no say in the matter. I like you, ghost. Wish you could be my friend."

"We are friends, Mr. Scrooge," the ghost replied. "You and me. All of us."

Scrooge drew in a deep breath, the crisp winter air refreshing his lungs. "As much as I'd like to continue this night of fun, I should return home to clean up. Not ideal to walk around with a man's blood on my clothes and skin. Just bad manners."

"Very well, sir."

The ghost spun and engulfed Scrooge without another word. The blackness consumed him, and instead of a freefall like their trip to this place, it felt like they were flying.

Flying to the top of the world. Well, Scrooge's apartment. Which often felt like the top of the world.

Scrooge landed in the hallway outside. Alone.

"Ghost?" he asked, feeling a pang of sadness. He really liked the last ghost and wished he could have stayed to chat. "Ghost, please come back!"

But no one answered. He looked down the hallway and saw the neighbor's door cracked open two inches. No light seeped out from the inside. As if the neighbor had left and forgotten to close the door. Pitch blackness.

While Scrooge was curious, he shook his head and returned to the confines of his own apartment. He danced as he entered, humming the tune of *Silent Night*.

Christmas isn't so bad, he thought. *Never knew it could be so fun.*

He took off his jacket and tossed it into the closet that concealed his washer and dryer. Then he danced his way to the bathroom, flicking on the light and studying the blood splatters across his face.

He smiled. "I don't even know whose blood that is! Could be Tim's or the girl's. Just delightful young people!"

Scrooge noticed the bloodstains on his top hat, frowned, then grinned again. He rather liked them. Added an extra touch. What did they call it in the fashion world? An accessory. Yes! Like sticking a feather in the ribbon around the base of the hat. The blood would stay. And if anyone asked what it was, well, they could fuck around and find out, as the kids said.

Scrooge ran to the sink and looked at himself in the mirror. The physical signs of age remained on his wrinkled face, but he saw the youth swimming behind his eyes. Not just youthfulness. But hope. This God forsaken holiday had ruined his life plenty of times in the past. But for the first time, Scrooge felt fully in control of Christmas. Spreading holiday doom and gloom was just what the doctor ordered.

He splashed water on his face and rubbed away the red stains, watching the bloody remains swirl away down the drain.

"A most fun night indeed!" Scrooge said to his reflection. "Looks like you still have plenty of energy left in the tank. Taking down two kids fifty years younger than you! Granted, one was a gimp. But still. Lots of life to live. More money to make. And more Christmases to spread holiday cheer."

The floor rumbled, and Scrooge thought it was the robot vacuum that would randomly go on a cleaning spree.

"Gloria?" he called out. That's what he named the robot. "Gloria, stop! Now's not the time for your antics."

But the steady hum and rumble continued.

Scrooge wiped his face dry and stormed out of the bathroom, ready to pick up Gloria and chuck her out the window.

But Gloria remained in her usual position along the baseboard in the living room. Turned off.

The ground trembled like an earthquake. Except nothing was moving within the apartment. If there were an earthquake, glasses would shake in the cupboards. The paintings would sway on the walls. None of that was happening, yet Scrooge still needed to hold on to the wall for fear of losing his balance.

"What the hell is going on?!" Scrooge cried out as the rumbling grew so intense he thought it was coming from within his head. Even leaning on the wall, he eventually fell to the floor, his top hat hanging crooked over his brow.

A beam of white light shot out of the living room floor. It started skinny, maybe six inches in diameter. Then it grew with each passing second, widening as the rumbling made it impossible for Scrooge to climb back to his feet. Surely the entire skyscraper was about to go down.

The light expanded to three feet wide and grew so bright Scrooge had to shield his eyes with his arm. A subtle movement from within the light had caught his attention, but it was too painful to look.

"Stop it!" Scrooge screamed, unable to hear himself over all the commotion.

Like the flick of a switch, the light vanished along with the rumbling.

Standing in Scrooge's living room was a new ghost, this one dressed in all white and glowing just as the light beam had.

It hovered, head and face concealed by immaculate white robes.

"Hello, sir," it said, this time a woman's voice. Gentle, almost caring.

"Wh-what are you?" Scrooge asked. "An angel?"

Surely the building had collapsed and Scrooge was dead, buried under a pile of rubble down below. Why else would an angel visit him?

"No, sir," the voice replied. "I'm the ghost of Christmas future. And I've come to show what will become of you. Hold my hand and fly with me."

"Fly?" Scrooge asked, and the ghost was already sticking out a hand from beneath its robes. This one wasn't frail like the last two had been. The hand in front of Scrooge even had flesh. He grabbed it and noted its softness. Like a warm, fluffy pillow.

"Never fear," the ghost said, and started rising, taking Scrooge with her. But before Scrooge could actually experience the thrill of flying, he became lightheaded, like someone had him in a choke hold. He was looking down at his living room from the ceiling before everything cut to darkness and his mind went completely blank.

He had no recollection of the time travel when he woke, standing on hard earth. Unlike his last two trips, where he felt the actual movement through time, this one was a blank slate when he came to.

Scrooge looked around. The skies were gray, the air brisk. Gravestones stood as far as he could see. A scatter of maple trees decorated the cemetery, bare and dormant, their branches black against the gloomy backdrop.

"What is this place?" Scrooge asked, knowing damn well what this all must mean.

"The finish line, Mr. Scrooge," the ghost replied in her motherly tone. "Come."

The ghost drifted behind Scrooge, causing him to spin around and see six rows behind him where a woman dressed in all black stood next to an open grave with a coffin about to be lowered into the ground.

Scrooge gulped as he followed the angel, not wanting to face this encounter. But he had no choice.

As he got closer, the woman standing at the grave looked up and made eye contact with Scrooge. He felt his heart sink, a sliver of panic creeping into his mind. The woman looked familiar but older.

"My God," she said, touching her lips with a gloved hand. She was short and pudgy, a lone pearl necklace providing the only color to her outfit.

As soon as she spoke, Scrooge recognized her voice at once. Susie Nash, the office manager from Cratchit and Dickens.

Scrooge stopped. "You can see me?" he asked.

"Of course," she said. "You must be his brother. Are you identical twins? Of course, he would have never told us that."

"I'm sorry," Scrooge said. "Whose brother?"

"You're obviously here for Ebenezer," she said, suspicion crawling over her face. "Are you not?"

Scrooge circled to stand by Susie and take in her view. His body froze when he saw the tombstone standing with his name on it.

Ebenezer Scrooge.

It gave the years of his life and had nothing else inscribed on the plain gray stone.

The temptation to raise the coffin's lid and look at his future dead self was too much. Fortunately for Scrooge, he couldn't move. His eyes were glued to the tombstone and coffin. The air was still like time had stopped.

"Did anyone else know about his funeral today?" Scrooge asked.

Susie sighed. "I'm afraid Ebenezer didn't have a big circle. In fact, we couldn't track down anyone from his personal life. He had no will, no records. It's a shame all of that money he had will get turned over to the government. Makes you wonder why he worked so hard to get it all, if he had no plan to leave it to someone."

This comment rubbed Scrooge the wrong way.

"Maybe it was what guided him through life," Scrooge said. "Not the money necessarily, but the pursuit of earning it. Gathering it."

"Kind of a sad life if you ask me," Susie said, shaking her head. "The entire office was informed of his death and invited to come out today. I know it's the day after Christmas, but still. No one wanted to, so I volunteered to come as our representative. Let's just say Ebenezer had a rocky relationship with everyone at work."

"So, I...Ebenezer dies, and you're the only one to show up at his funeral?" Scrooge asked. "What would happen if you didn't come?"

Susie shrugged. "I suppose the caretaker would have just lowered him into the ground and buried him. It's a shame, isn't it? Coming to the end of your life and having no one mourn your death."

"Are you mourning?" Scrooge asked.

Susie looked at the coffin as if recalling the several memories she had with Scrooge. If you could call them that. She finally shook her head. "I won't speak ill of the dead, but Ebenezer and I butted heads plenty of times. I was only ever trying to be nice. It'll be...*different*, not having him around. But I can't go as far as saying I'll miss him. He made my life plenty difficult, unfortunately."

Scrooge nodded as if accepting this articulate response, but deep down his fire raged. Having Susie be the only one to show up at his funeral was more of a slap in the face than if no one had come.

"So you *are* his brother, right?" Susie asked. "I don't mean to make assumptions, but when I saw you walking over, I thought you were him for a second."

"Something like that, yes."

Scrooge balled his fists. He had nothing but anger at his disposal. No dining table full of potential weapons. No bum's gun to use.

"You bitch," Scrooge muttered under his breath.

"I beg your pardon!" Susie cried out.

Just as she turned to look at him, Scrooge whipped his hands out from his jacket pockets and squeezed them around Susie's throat.

Susie grabbed on to Scrooge's wrists and attempted to pull his hands off. She was no match for Scrooge's adrenaline-filled strength. Guttural noises came from her throat as her face turned bright pink, and eventually purple.

A plump plum, Scrooge thought, laughing in his thoughts.

"You were nothing more than a pain in my ass," Scrooge said, their noses inches apart. "Always in my business, trying to figure out what I was working on. Offering up mindless interns to assist me. Like I ever needed assistance! Why couldn't you just back off and order coffee cups for the office like you were supposed to?!"

Scrooge squeezed harder, and Susie's hands fell limply to her sides. Her eyes remained open, puffing out of their sockets as they turned bloodshot.

"If no one's going to remember me," Scrooge said. "Then the world will forget you by tonight."

He spat in her face and held her throat for another ten seconds until she fell out of his grip as she became dead weight. Susie collapsed to the frigid ground and lay in a pile of chunky limbs.

"Thought you could buy your way to heaven coming to my funeral?" Scrooge asked her lifeless body. "Burn in hell!"

He always wanted to tell her that, but knew he couldn't in the office. The human resources people would have a field day with that. Those spineless fucks.

Scrooge bent down and grabbed Susie by her wrists, tugging her arms until she untangled and lay flat on her back. He yanked, grunting with each attempt to pull her body. The bitch was as heavy as she looked.

It took him ten minutes, but he finally got her to the edge of the grave. She lay beneath the coffin elevated on the casket lowering device.

Scrooge dropped to a knee, panting for breath. "Whatever alternate reality this is, you can enjoy your afterlife beneath me, as you belong."

He shoved Susie with all his might. Her body rolled in slow motion, falling into the grave with a thunderous bang when she hit the bottom of the hole.

Scrooge climbed to his feet and looked into the grave. Susie lay down there, splayed out, her head bobbing from side to side.

"Shit!" Scrooge cried. He patted his pockets, hoping he had a gun by chance. But he did not.

That left him with one choice.

He hurried to the crank handle on the lowering device and started spinning it furiously. The coffin containing his future body rocked on the straps as it descended jerkily into the earth. He kept cranking the handle, even after the straps had fallen into the grave.

It took him a minute to realize he was done. He stopped, gasping for fresh air, then shuffled to the edge of the grave and looked down.

It had been dug perfectly to fit the casket, and he noticed it tilted at the slightest of angles from being on top of Susie's body. But he didn't think it was enough to raise the suspicions of whichever poor soul had to come and refill this hole.

And even if they noticed something off, would they actually climb down there and do anything about it? The casket was deep enough to proceed with the burial as normal. And as long as Susie didn't make a sound, nobody would ever know she was down there.

The casket would weigh at least two hundred pounds. With her already having no strength, he couldn't imagine her returning to full consciousness. That amount of weight would eventually crush her lungs. Or at the least, make it incredibly difficult to breathe, let alone shout something.

Scrooge wiped sweat from his brow and spun around to find the glowing white ghost hovering in the distance. He looked back down in the grave. "So long, old friend," he said. "I suppose we'll do this again someday, in the real world."

The ghost floated up next to Scrooge and looked into the grave with him. "Is everything finished here, Mr. Scrooge?"

Scrooge gazed at his tombstone one last time and wondered why no one else had come to his funeral.

Assholes.

"Yes, ghost," he said. "Everything is perfect."

Who Goes There?

THE GHOST OF CHRISTMAS future returned Scrooge to his apartment and left him in a silent peace before departing.

Scrooge sat on the couch in his living room and couldn't remember the last time he had done such a thing. His routine usually included going to the office, coming home and eating at the kitchen table, working for a few hours in his home office, then eventually going to bed.

Sitting on the couch would imply having nothing to do. Having no money to make. Why even entertain such a thought?

But as he sat there now, the air from the heater blowing the curtains apart enough to glimpse New York City below, Scrooge had never felt more accomplished. Forget the bank account that had two commas in it. The luxurious apartment was a mere bonus in life. What Scrooge did tonight was more important than any of that.

He avenged his mother's death, and eliminated people who didn't understand him. He wondered if any of it had actually happened. It all felt so real. Hell, his feet were still thawing after spending the last hour at that frozen cemetery.

"It can't have been real," Scrooge said to his empty living room. "There is no such thing as ghosts or time travel. Tiny Tim and Susie will be in the office after Christmas and we can all go back to our misery."

He looked at the TV hanging on the wall. Again, something he hadn't used in at least two years, but he had bought it because it seemed like the right thing to do. He grabbed the remote and clicked on the TV, which opened to a local news station.

A young Black woman spoke from somewhere on the streets in Manhattan, the bright lights casting a glow across her face.

Scrooge noticed the headline: MANHUNT UNDERWAY. FOUR PEOPLE DEAD.

That grabbed his attention, so he cranked up the volume.

"A homeless man was found shot in the head tonight, right outside a local café where he was believed to be sleeping on the curb."

Scrooge recognized the background behind the field reporter. It was the same café he had passed on his way home from work. But was it the same homeless man he had insulted?

"Another block down," the reporter said. "A hat store was broken into. The store's owner reports no money was taken, and from what they could tell by a quick glance, no inventory was missing. Traffic cameras caught this fuzzy image of a man crossing the intersection minutes after the store's alarm had been tripped."

The screen changed to show a blurred, still image of a tall man crossing the street, wearing a dark top hat. Scrooge removed the hat from his head and stared at it.

"Authorities find it hard to believe someone would have broken in to steal one hat," the reporter said. "But both matters are under investigation."

Scrooge drew in a deep breath. His heart was racing, hands sweating as he stared at the hat. He had opened that present. Touched the box with his bare hands in an alleyway, and placed it on his head. He hadn't broken into a hat store...

He put the hat down on the couch next to him, its bloody stains dried up.

"There's more to unfold," the reporter continued. "It's been quite the Christmas Eve around New York. A couple was found dead in their home in Brooklyn tonight. The names of the victims have not been released, but police are describing it as a horrific scene inside the house. They appeared to have been eating dinner, as there was still food and drink on the table. The big mystery concerns a third plate that appeared to be untouched. The couple did not have a camera doorbell or any other security measures. FBI agents are expected to question everyone in the neighborhood."

Scrooge's heart thumped madly. His throat dried up.

"It was all real," he whispered.

"And the last bit of news," the anchor said. Scrooge already knew what was coming. "Susie Nash from Brooklyn was found dead in her backyard with bruises around her throat. She worked for the financial firm, Cratchit and Dickens, and lived alone. Authorities believe she was choked to death in her home before being dragged out to her backyard."

Scrooge's mind spun out of control. How could everyone he killed while traveling through time actually be dead? It wasn't supposed to work that way. He couldn't simply spend the rest of his days in prison for something he hadn't known he was actually doing. You couldn't convict someone for murdering in their dreams.

"This has been a terrifying night across New York City," the anchor said. "Authorities are investigating if there is any link between all the crimes. If anyone has a tip, please reach out to your local police department. As of now, there are no suspects. Stay safe out there, and try to enjoy the Christmas holiday."

The segment ended, and Scrooge turned off the TV, jumping up from the couch, feeling like he might vomit all over his apartment. His hands trembled violently beyond his control. It felt like the walls were closing in on him. Any minute, someone would come knocking on his door. Only this time, it wouldn't be a ghost. It would be an FBI agent to arrest him and throw him in jail while they sorted all this out.

"If I'm lucky, they'll only tie the hat to me. I don't have that gun anymore, and there's no proof I was in either of those houses tonight. Because I wasn't!"

He looked at the top hat on the couch and considered how the bloodstains could have gotten on it. When he thought back to the evening, all he could remember were the three ghosts taking him to different places so that he could do his deeds. Spread the holiday cheer, one might say.

"It wasn't supposed to be real!" he cried, panting like a dehydrated dog. "I never actually left this apartment tonight. I've been in here the whole time."

"But it is real," a voice said from the bathroom. *His* voice. "And you *did* leave tonight."

"Who goes there?!" Scrooge shouted. "Show yourself!"

"You've already shown yourself tonight," the voice said. It was calm, yet authoritative.

Scrooge darted into the kitchen and grabbed a knife from the rack on the counter. "You have three seconds to step out and face me like a man!"

No response.

"One...two...THREE!" Scrooge shouted and ran down the hallway to the bathroom, barreling through the doorway and slashing the knife through the air before even turning on the light.

The blade met nothing, so Scrooge reached over and turned on the light switch. The bathroom was empty.

"You really need to calm down," the voice said, and Scrooge jumped at the sight of his reflection in the mirror speaking to him.

He looked into the mirror, brushing a hand against his face. The reflection did not mimic his movements as it should.

Instead, the mirror version of Scrooge only stood there with his arms crossed, an evil glare stuck on his face.

"This isn't real," Scrooge said, backing away from the mirror until his legs hit the toilet.

The reflection grinned. "It's all real, my friend. Real as you and me."

"*You're* not real!" Scrooge shouted. He balled a fist and punched the mirror. The cracks webbed out from the area of impact, yet the reflection remained with its mad grin.

"Oh, Ebenezer," the reflection said, shaking his head. "I've always been a part of you. I've lived within you. Roaming the back halls of your mind, if you will. You don't actually believe you reached this point in life on your own, do you? That's not fair to me."

"Of course I did," Scrooge said, no longer fearing the reflection speaking to him, but embracing this as a mental breakdown of sorts. Yes, that was the only explanation.

"Oh, Ebenezer," the reflection replied. "When you lost your mother, a new chapter began in your life. Me. When we met, you were nothing but a shy, terrified little boy. Your beautiful, complicated mind created me to help you cope. And once you came to terms with your new reality, we really began to have some fun. You let me out of the cage. Off the leash. Use whichever metaphor you'd like, but without me, you'd still be that scared little boy. Probably stuck at some entry-level accounting job for the rest of your life. Too afraid to take a risk."

"I'm self-made!" Scrooge barked, growing furious with the reflection downplaying his entire life.

"Ha!" The reflection widened his mad grin. "No one reaches your level of success on their own. There is no such thing! How many necks did you have to step on to get where you are? How many shady, off-the-record dealings did you make when no one was looking? Don't stand there and act like every penny in your bank account is legitimate. You've ripped people off. Have you ever even tipped any of the food delivery people?"

"A tip?!" Scrooge cried. "I've never tipped for something I can do myself. Preposterous! We all have our jobs to do. No one has ever tipped me for making them millionaires."

"Right," the reflection replied. "You just raise your commission by a fraction every year so that they'll never actually notice. That's illegal, my friend. You don't even disclose it. But that's besides the point—it was my idea, after all."

The reflection laughed.

"What is so funny?" Scrooge demanded.

"You, Ebenezer. You've always been so lost in this world. But you could always hide behind the money. And up here in your skyrise bunker. Do you really not know who lives in the other apartment on this floor?"

Scrooge shook his head. "Of course not. I've never seen anyone."

"Oh, Ebenezer," the reflection said. "Why don't you head over right now? I'll meet you there."

Just You and Me

SCROOGE STOOD OUTSIDE THE other apartment door. It was still a couple of inches ajar, a cold draft seeping through the gap.

This is mad, he thought. *All the other illusions...or whatever they were. Those can be explained. Exhaustion? Or, dare I think, old age? The marbles can be rattling around. But this? I have no business bothering my kind neighbor who has never bothered me.*

He knocked on the door, and it opened another three inches.

"Hello?" Scrooge called out. "Is anyone home?"

Silence.

Of course no one is home. Because I've never seen anyone on this floor. No one lives here.

His heart rate grew rapid, sweat forming around his brow. He took off the top hat to wipe it away.

"Hello?" he cried out. "My name is Ebenezer Scrooge. I'm your neighbor from down the hall."

Silence.

"I only want to meet whoever lives in this apartment."

Silence.

"God dammit," Scrooge muttered. He pushed the door all the way open, revealing complete darkness. "No one's even here."

He stepped in and reached around the wall for the light switch. When he turned it on, he froze in confusion.

The floor plan was identical to his own apartment. That much was expected for two units on the same floor. But what disturbed Scrooge was the furniture and decorations inside.

It was all the same as his apartment. Same dining table. Couch. TV. Only the artwork was different, although the pieces hung in the exact locations as his apartment.

"What the hell?" Scrooge said, looking around and feeling as if his head might explode.

"I'm back here!" the voice from his reflection called, echoing all around the empty apartment. "In the office."

Scrooge jumped, startled by the unexpected voice calling out to him. *His* voice.

He rubbed his forehead. *In the office.* Like he knew where that was. But he did.

"I'm dreaming. Soon, I'll wake up in my bed. In *my* apartment. And I'll just go to work. Anywhere but here."

Convinced the last several hours were a mere figment of his imagination, Scrooge went down the hallway and entered his office. When he turned on the light, he spotted himself sitting at the desk.

It was no longer a reflection. No. It was really him, typing on the computer and grumbling inaudible words under his breath.

The carbon copy of Scrooge turned around and stood up, clapping his hands together. "I didn't think you'd actually come. Guess you have some courage on your own. Great to know!"

"What is this place?" Scrooge asked, looking around to see the office set up identical to his own.

"Like I said earlier—before you punched me, I might add—I've always been with you. A part of you, Ebenezer. Anything bad you've ever done, that has any type of evidence, is hidden here. No one lives here, dumbass! You own this apartment. I made you buy it when you moved into the building."

"Nonsense!" Scrooge replied. "I've never stepped foot in this apartment."

"You didn't buy this apartment under your name," the second Scrooge continued, an evil grin touching his lips. "I'm not that stupid. You used Marley's identification to buy this place. No one would ever have a reason to search this apartment if you found yourself in deep trouble. Which you might, after tonight."

"Marley?" Scrooge asked.

"Yes, Jacob Marley," second Scrooge said. "Your BFF, as the kids say. Best friend forever. We'll take that to heart. You have his social security card, birth certificate, death certificate. All of it. He, like you, had no family to leave anything to, remember? You got it all because you were the only person in his life. And that's where I came in."

"To buy this place to...do my dirty work?" Scrooge asked.

"No, sir. No dirty work happens here. It is only *stored* here. Now, I wanted to get a storage unit outside of town. Preferably off Manhattan. But you refused. Never wanted to have to drive so far. Not sure why you have so many nice cars in that garage downstairs, but that's beside the point. So I had to get more creative. And what better place than right down the hallway? Now you essentially own this entire floor. No visitors. No foot traffic. Just you, yourself, and me!"

"I see nothing out of the ordinary," Scrooge said, crossing his arms. "If you have evidence of anything wrong I've done, as you claim, I'd notice it."

Second Scrooge laughed. "Ebby, Ebby, Ebby. Do you take me for a fool? Would I leave a smoking gun on the kitchen table? Come on."

He marched past Scrooge and turned down the hallway into the bedroom, which was identical to his actual bedroom next door.

Scrooge followed him into the closet, which was complete with the same wardrobe hanging on the rack, but there was one difference from his actual closet.

This one had a filing cabinet tucked into the corner.

"Just something for storage," the second Scrooge said.

Scrooge paused to gawk at the filing cabinet. What could this imaginary version of himself possibly have in it?

I've already come this far. Why not keep playing along?

"You should be so lucky," the faux Scrooge said. "I'm always there to clean up your messes. Like tonight. You sure did put me to work. Shooting a bum on the sidewalk. All it would have taken was one witness, and this night would be completely different. Still, I made sure you picked up the spent round and brought the gun back here."

Second Scrooge shuffled over to the filing cabinet and pulled open the drawer. He reached in and pulled out the silver revolver he had used on the homeless man. Then he grabbed a small pouch from the cabinet, opened it, and fished out the spent round. He held it high and shined the light on it as if it were the holy grail.

"See," he said. "Covered your ass. I also cut the camera feed at the hat store. Saved you there. And took the steak knife and wineglass from Tim's house. You fool! You actually tossed the glass back on his dead body, covered with your fingerprints and DNA. Like you were just begging to be caught. I picked that up, too, on our way out."

He slipped the gun into his inner coat pocket, then returned to the cabinet to pull out the broken wineglass he had stabbed Tim in the gut with.

"This can't be," Scrooge said, his eyes narrowed on the wineglass. Anything else could have been replicated. The gun. The spent round. Even the steak knife. But the wineglass and its specific jagged edges.

That couldn't have been faked. There was even dried blood around its zigzagged rim.

The other Scrooge put the glass back inside the drawer and slammed it shut. "It's all here, Ebby. Deposit slips from your little bank account in the Cayman Islands. The paperwork from opening those accounts, and all the other questionable accounts you've used for your backdoor dealings. It's all safe and sound in the apartment no one will ever search. Would you like to leave your new top hat in here? It's covered with DNA that will absolutely incriminate you."

Scrooge barely heard the question, his mind spinning out of control. He couldn't deny the proof in front of his eyes. This wasn't made up. Or a dream.

It had all happened. The bum. Tiny Tim and his lady friend. And Susie. She was really dead!

The realization left him dazed, struggling to grasp how it all played out. Yes, he had shot a homeless man, but that was in the past. And if it wasn't, then he must have suffered through some sort of illusion. A *violent* illusion. One scenario played out in his mind while another occurred in reality. Was such a thing even possible?

"It's possible," the other Scrooge said. "And it happened. Christmas broke you, my friend. After all these years of misery it caused you, the damned holiday finally split your sanity right in half."

"No," Scrooge said, backing away. He needed to get out of this apartment.

"And I couldn't sit by and watch you suffer any more. Your suffering is my suffering. We're forever intertwined."

"No," Scrooge repeated, shaking his head, turning to run out of the closet.

"You killed those people," the other Scrooge said from the closet doorway.

Scrooge halted in his tracks, looking back at the filing cabinet, then back to the other Scrooge in front of him. "How did you?"

The other Scrooge laughed. "Ebby. It's just you and me. Always has been. Always will be. I had enough of watching you get mentally destroyed every Christmas. So I thought, why don't we fight back? Christmas has broken us, so let's break Christmas."

He'd never planned to kill anyone. Fantasized about it? Sure. Especially Susie. How he'd have loved to push her down an elevator shaft. But everyone had those dark thoughts from time to time. Regular people didn't actually act on them.

"You're not regular, Ebby," the other Scrooge said. "*We're* not regular. And you know the best part? We can do this every year. It can be our little secret. I'll always help you get rid of the evidence."

The other Scrooge reached into his jacket pocket and pulled out the same gun he—they?—had used earlier on the bum. He held it out, hand over the barrel so Scrooge could grab the grip. "Every year," he repeated.

Scrooge stared at the gun. Whoever this other version of himself was wouldn't go away. The ghosts would be back. He knew it. A grin gradually spread over Scrooge's face. He straightened his top hat and grabbed the gun.

He whipped the gun forward, aiming it at the other version of himself. "You're not real," Scrooge whispered. "None of this is real."

Second Scrooge grinned madly. "Shooting me won't make me go away. I may not be a physical thing you can touch. But, my friend, I am real. As real as the ghosts who all visited tonight. And they'll be back. Every year. I promise."

Scrooge tightened his finger around the trigger, every fiber in his body begging him to pull it. But the other version of him was right. Christmas had been breaking his spirit every year since he was a child.

Why don't I ever get to enjoy the holiday?

Scrooge loosened his finger from the trigger and smiled.

"Alright, let's make Christmas merry again."

Twisted Tales of Familiar Faces

If you enjoyed this horror retelling of *A Christmas Carol*, don't miss out on the rest of this horrifying collection!

Humbug (Scrooge) - Andre Gonzalez

Sweethaven (Popeye) - RJ Clark

Timber Beast (Paul Bunyan) - A.K. Hughey

Alice (Alice in Wonderland) - Audrey Brice

Wish (Aladdin) - Courtney Konstantin

Quixote (Don Quixote) - Stephen Wertzbaugher

Arturius (King Arthur) - A.K. Hughey

Steamboat (Steamboat Willie) - Courtney Konstantin

Strangled (Rapunzel) - Stephen Wertzbaugher

Dethroning Oz (Wizard of Oz) - Audrey Brice

Scorned (Hercules) - Z.S. Diamanti

Check out the entire collection at www.m4lpublishing.com

Join our newsletter to stay up to date with all upcoming releases at www.m4lpublishing.com

Author's Note

I had an idea one night regarding public domain characters. With all the horror remakes I've seen coming out, mainly Winnie the Pooh and Steamboat Willie (yes, these are actual horror movies now), I dug into public domain rules and what it all means.

Basically, any work of fiction that has entered the public domain is fair to use in other works. I noticed Popeye was hitting the public domain in 2025, and my idea was to create a Popeye horror story to release at the start of 2025 and take advantage.

The idea itself was good (and you're probably wondering what Popeye has to do with my book about Scrooge, but keep reading), but not good enough for my wife and business partner, Natasha. When I floated this idea to her, she took it and made it much bigger than I intended, as she does with pretty much any idea that floats out of my head.

The very next day she was on phone calls all day with several of our horror author friends, asking if they'd have any interest in writing a horror story based on public domain characters.

Sure enough, they had interest, and now an entire collective was born. With a plethora of characters to choose from now, I decided to take on Ebenezer Scrooge instead of Popeye. I handed Popeye off to the talented RJ Clark. That book is titled *Sweethaven and* is the second in this collection.

Something about Scrooge called to me. I'd done Christmas horror before (see Snowball), and have built a career off time travel. This was a unique opportunity to combine both avenues into one story, so I couldn't resist. Besides, what could be more than taking a story about redemption and turning into one of revenge? Maybe that's just my inner horror writer, but it was an absolute blast having Scrooge hate Christmas and setting him free to continue down that path.

I hope you enjoyed this story as much as I did writing it. I'll admit it was hard for me, after writing several books in the 100,000-word range, to work on a story that needed to fall between 20,000-40,000. But being forced to write tighter only improves the quality of words on the page, much to my chagrin.

A few thank yous are in order. First off, to Melissa Prideaux for once again lending a critical and incredibly helpful during the editing process. It's wild how a few minor tweaks can strengthen everything.

Thank you to the authors who were so gracious to trust us publishing their work for this first round (yes, there will be more). RJ, Stephanie, Audrey, Courtney, Stephen, and Zach...let's do this!

As always, I owe a thank you to my kids, Arielle, Felix, and Selena. You're all getting older and seeing how this publishing life works. I appreciate the questions and the motivation you provide daily.

And last, to Natasha. For bringing my silly idea into a fully blown collective to help grow our publishing house. Not only did you make all the covers (no easy task), you have spear-headed this project entirely...just like I requested (hey, I just wanted to do one book!).

The future is now incredibly bright for us at M4L Publishing, and I can't wait to see how big this collective will grow. Onward and upward!

Enjoy this book?

We hope you enjoyed this release from M4L Publishing.

Reviews are the most helpful tools in getting new readers for any books. We don't have the financial backing of a New York publishing house and can't afford to blast our books on billboards or bus stops.

(Not yet!)

That said, your honest review can go a long way in helping us reach new readers. If you've enjoyed this book, we'd be forever grateful if you could spend a couple minutes leaving it a review (it can be as short as you like) on the site you purchased this book from.

Thank you so much!

About the author

Andre Gonzalez is the international bestselling author of the *Wealth of Time Series*, and co-owner of M4L Publishing.

After surviving the Aurora Theater Shooting in 2012, Andre was inspired to chase his lifelong dream of pursuing a career as an author. This tragedy gave him a new appreciation for life along with a drive to make the world a better place by publishing books readers all around the world can enjoy.

He has written over twenty time-travel, thriller, and horror books after spending many years reading and studying the works of Stephen King and Dean Koontz. Keeping readers up late and their hearts pumping faster than normal is his ultimate goal. Andre was the recipient of the Rocky Mountain Fiction Writers 2021 Independent Writer of the Year award.

When he's not writing, you can find Andre buried underneath a long to-do list or chasing around his three hyper children. He and his wife are raising their family in their hometown of Denver, CO.

Author Website: www.andregonzalez.net